DAN THE ANT

By Jennifer B. Gillis
Illustrated by Karen Stormer Brooks

BARRON'S

Table of Contents

Illustrations on pages 21–23 created by Carol Stutz

All inquiries should be addressed to:
Barron's Educational Series, Inc.
250 Wireless Boulevard
Hauppauge, New York 11788
www.barronseduc.com

Library of Congress Catalog Card No.: 2005053583

ISBN-13: 978-0-7641-3282-7
ISBN-10: 0-7641-3282-2

Library of Congress Cataloging-in-Publication Data
Gillis, Jennifer Blizin, 1950–
    Dan the ant / Jennifer B. Gillis.
       p. cm. – (Reader's clubhouse)
    ISBN-13: 978-0-7641-3282-7
    ISBN-10: 0-7641-3282-2
    1. Ants—Juvenile literature. I. Title. II. Series.

QL568.F7G42 2006
595.79'6—dc22

                                                                2005053583

PRINTED IN CHINA
9 8 7 6 5 4 3 2 1

Dear Parent and Educator,

Welcome to the Barron's Reader's Clubhouse, a series of books that provide a phonics approach to reading.

Phonics is the relationship between letters and sounds. It is a system that teaches children that letters have specific sounds. Level 1 books introduce the short-vowel sounds. Level 2 books progress to the long-vowel sounds. This progression matches how phonics is taught in many classrooms.

Dan the Ant introduces the short "a" sound. Simple words with this short-vowel sound are called **decodable words.** The child knows how to sound out these words because he or she has learned the sound they include. This story also contains **high-frequency words.** These are common, everyday words that the child learns to read by sight. High-frequency words help ensure fluency and comprehension. **Challenging words** go a little beyond the reading level. The child will identify these words with help from the illustration on the page. All words are listed by their category on page 24.

Here are some coaching and prompting statements you can use to help a young reader read *Dan the Ant:*

- **On page 4, "Dan" is a decodable word. Point to the word and say:**

  Read this word. How did you know the word? What sounds did it make?

  Note: There are many opportunities to repeat the above instruction throughout the book.

- **On page 7, "snack" is a challenging word. Point to the word and say:**

  Read this word. It rhymes with "back." How did you know the word? Did you look at the pictures? How did they help?

You'll find more coaching ideas on the Reader's Clubhouse Web site: *www.barronsclubhouse.com.* Reader's Clubhouse is designed to teach and reinforce reading skills in a fun way. We hope you enjoy helping children discover their love of reading!

Sincerely,

Nancy Harris

Nancy Harris
Reading Consultant

This is Dan the Ant.

Dan is sad.

Dan likes snacks.

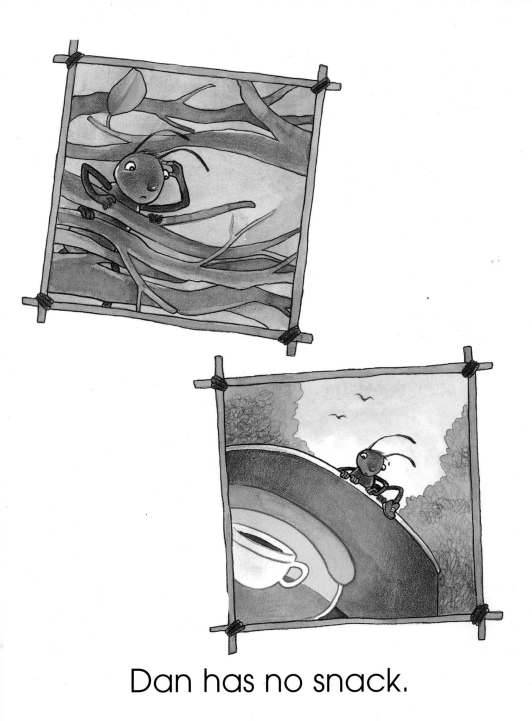

Dan has no snack.

Dan can see a bag.

There is a snack in the bag.

Dan must get to the bag.

Dan makes a map.

Dan makes a path.

It is a path to a ramp.

Dan is on the ramp.

Dan gets the snack.

It is jam.

Dan likes the snack.

Dan is not a sad ant.

Dan is a glad ant.

Fun Facts About
Ants

- There are more than 8,000 different kinds of ants in the world.

- Ants can lift things 50 times heavier than they are.

- Ants can organize groups to carry extremely heavy things.

- Ants have very strong jaws called mandibles.

- Ants use their antennae to touch, taste, and smell things.

Ants on a Log

Here are some ants that you can eat.
Ask an adult to help you.

You will need:
- celery stalks
- cream cheese or peanut butter
- raisins

1. Rinse the celery. Dry it with a paper towel. Ask an adult to cut each stalk into two or three pieces.

2. Use a butter knife to spread the cream cheese or peanut butter into the hollow part of each celery stick.

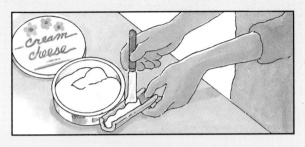

3. Put a line of raisins on top of the cream cheese or peanut butter.

4. Eat and enjoy your ants on a log!

Word List

Challenging Words	path snack snacks	
Short A Decodable Words	ant bag can Dan glad has jam map	ramp sad
High-Frequency Words	a get gets in is it likes makes must no not on the there	this to